A Fairy Ballet

Pearl
the Cloud Fairy

Abigail
the Breeze Fairy

Goldie
the Sunshine Fairy

The Weather Fairies

Hayley
the Rain Fairy

Crystal
the Snow Fairy

Storm
the Lightning Fairy

Evie
the Mist Fairy

Library of Congress Cataloging-in-Publication Data is available.

ISBN 978-0-545-22294-5

10 9 8 7 6 5 4 3   11 12 13 14/0

Printed in the U.S.A.   40
First printing, March 2011

A Fairy Ballet

by Daisy Meadows

SCHOLASTIC INC.

New York   Toronto   London   Auckland

Sydney   Mexico City   New Delhi   Hong Kong

It's early morning in Fairyland, and the Weather Fairies are just waking up. There's a loud knock at their door. "Who could it be?" Crystal wonders.

Storm opens the door, and a frog strides in.
It's Bertram, the royal messenger.

"Hello, Weather Fairies," Bertram says. "I have an invitation from the Fairy Godmother for you."

"The Fairy Godmother?" gasps Evie.

Goldie opens the envelope and reads:

Dear fairies and friends:
Come one, come all!
In Fairyland, we will have a ball.
With songs and skits
for the king and queen,
it will be a celebration
like you've never seen.
Please be sure to prepare your part.
Bring a gift straight from your heart.
It's a night of fun for all to share.
I hope that I will see you there.

Always,
Fairy Godmother

"Oh, it sounds wonderful," sighs Hayley. "But what about the gift?" Abigail asks.

"The Fairy Godmother wants the guests to perform for the king and queen," Bertram explains. "That will be your gift. Remember, it needs to be from the heart."

The Weather Fairies look at one another.
"Have a good day," Bertram says. "See you at
the party."

"I can't believe we have to perform for the king and queen," says Crystal.

"We'll think of something," Goldie says.

"It has to be from the heart," Hayley reminds them.

Just then, a beautiful song dances
through the window.
"Let's go outside," suggests Crystal.
"We do our best thinking there."

Outside, the fairies see a bird.
"Was that your pretty song?" Pearl asks
the bird.

The bird chirps and flies toward the forest.
The fairies follow.

"I love to hear the breeze whisper," Abigail says.
"I love how things look magical in the mist,"
says Evie.

"Well, *I* love snowflakes," says Crystal.
"When I watch them whirl around, I want
to dance."
"We all love weather," Goldie says.
"Maybe that can be our gift."

"How?" asks Storm.

"We can dance to show everyone how weather makes us feel," says Goldie.

"We can create a ballet!" Evie exclaims.

All the fairies are excited, except Crystal.

"I'm not so sure," Crystal says quietly.

"But why?" Storm asks. "You love to dance."

"I like to dance for me," Crystal explains.

"But what if I mess up?"

"You'll be fine," Goldie insists.

"We'll practice. We're all in this together."
Crystal tries to smile.

Each fairy plans a special dance for her kind of weather.
Then they all work on the grand dance that comes at the end of their ballet.

"We're all in the finale," Hayley says.
"Because it's a gift from all of us."

The fairies start to practice.

They help one another with their dances.
Each one is different, but they all tell a story
about weather.

When it is Crystal's turn, she is nervous.
Before her big leap, she stumbles and falls.

"I'll never get it right," Crystal says with a
sigh. "I can't dance in front of the king and
queen."

Abigail helps the snow fairy up.
"Don't worry about them," Evie suggests.
"When you dance from the heart, you
won't even know the crowd is there."

"I've seen you do that leap hundreds of
times," Hayley says. "You just have to
believe in yourself, like we believe in you."
Crystal nods and starts her dance again.

The Weather Fairies practice and practice. They also design and sew their costumes.

Then they meet with the fairy orchestra.
A ballet needs music!

The night of the Fairy Godmother's
party arrives.
There is a big outdoor stage.

The guests sit on blankets under the stars.
The Fairy Godmother, King Oberon, and
Queen Titania are there.

The Weather Fairies wait for their turn
backstage.
Crystal peeks out from behind the curtain
and crosses her wings for good luck.

The fairy orchestra starts to play the ballet music.

Goldie is the first to go on. She does a dance of the rising sun. At first, the stage is dark. Then rays of light burst from Goldie's wand as she dances.

Pearl bounds in next, flipping from one fluffy cloud to another.

Storm's dance is like lightning: bold, fast, and flashy.

Hayley wears rain boots and dances with an umbrella, twirling in a dizzy spin.

Then Evie dances onto the stage, slow and graceful, like a misty dream.

Abigail wears a crown of acorns, and skips as she throws leaves in the air like the autumn breeze.

The music grows soft.
Giant, glittery snowflakes begin to fall.
Crystal floats onto the stage, whirling
around with the snowflakes.

It's time for her big jump. Crystal leaps
into the air. When she lands, she's so
happy, she glows.

The seven fairies dance onto the stage for the finale.
Their wings sparkle under the starry sky.

The music fills their hearts, and they pirouette around the stage.
With a swirl of their wands, the sky lights up with weather magic!

The Weather Fairies bow, and the Fairy
Godmother hurries onto the stage.
"What a beautiful ballet!" she exclaims.
"We did it!" Goldie says to her fairy sisters.
Crystal smiles. "Yes, we danced straight
from the heart."

Dear Family and Friends of New Readers,

Welcome to Scholastic Reader. We have taken over ninety years' worth of experience with teachers, parents, and children and put it into a program that is designed to match your child's interest and skills. Each Scholastic Reader is designed to support your child's efforts to learn how to read at every age and every stage.

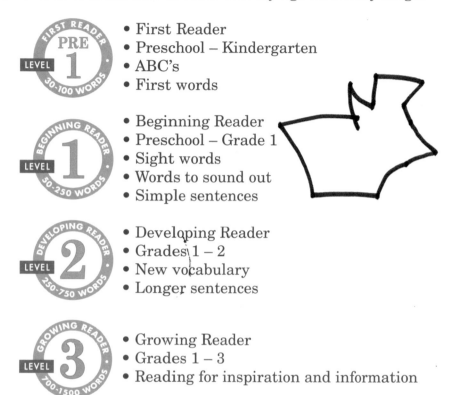

FIRST READER · PRE LEVEL 1 · 30-100 WORDS
- First Reader
- Preschool – Kindergarten
- ABC's
- First words

BEGINNING READER · LEVEL 1 · 50-250 WORDS
- Beginning Reader
- Preschool – Grade 1
- Sight words
- Words to sound out
- Simple sentences

DEVELOPING READER · LEVEL 2 · 250-750 WORDS
- Developing Reader
- Grades 1 – 2
- New vocabulary
- Longer sentences

GROWING READER · LEVEL 3 · 700-1500 WORDS
- Growing Reader
- Grades 1 – 3
- Reading for inspiration and information

On the back of every book, we have indicated the grade level, guided reading level, Lexile® level, and word count. You can use this information to find a book that is a good fit for your child.

For ideas about sharing books with your new reader, please visit www.scholastic.com. Enjoy helping your child learn to read and love to read!

Happy Reading!

—**Francie Alexander**
Chief Academic Officer
Scholastic Inc.

The Weather Fairies
perform a ballet—
straight from the heart!

LEVEL PRE 1 — FIRST READER — 30-100 WORDS
ABC's & first words.

LEVEL 1 — BEGINNING READER — 50-250 WORDS
Sight words, words to sound out & simple sentences.

LEVEL 2 — DEVELOPING READER — 250-750 WORDS
New vocabulary & longer sentences.

LEVEL 3 — GROWING READER — 700-1500 WORDS
Reading for inspiration & information.

Based on the best research about how children learn to read, Scholastic Readers are developed under the supervision of reading experts and are educator approved.

DEVELOPING READER	GRADE LEVEL	GUIDED READING LEVEL		
Level 2	Grade 1-2	M	500L	847

BK04469624

ISBN 978-0-545-22294-5
EAN
9 780545 222945
50399